Dear Parent,

Moving from being a non-reader to a reader is one of the most magical transitions in life. For some children, it happens with lightening speed. For others, more slowly. Whatever your child's experience may be, the best way to encourage reading ability is to focus on the enjoyment and fun of a story.

Here are some ways to support success:

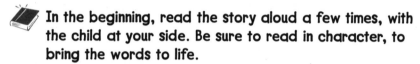

In the beginning, read the story aloud a few times, with the child at your side. Be sure to read in character, to bring the words to life.

Run your finger under the text as you read to help the child connect printed and spoken words. Before you know it, he or she will be participating in the reading.

Let the child fill in words as you read through the book, especially predictable or repeated phrases or words that complete rhymes.

If the child tries to sound out words, encourage the activity—but never force a child to struggle unduly with a word. Just say the word, let him or her repeat it, and move on.

As you read, allow your child to linger on a page as long as he or she likes, examining the pictures or discussing the story with you.

First and foremost, share in the fun and excitement of the story. Realizing that reading is fun **is** your child's first step toward becoming a reader!

For Sam, Cassie, and Luke—
C.L.

To Chester, Emily, Cindy, Marissa,
Valerie, Cody, Taylor and "Nolly".......
for keeping me young with their precious,
and sometimes toothless, smiles.
S.S.

© 2002 Gruner + Jahr USA Publishing
All Rights Reserved. Produced under License
by Learning Horizons, Inc.

Parents Magazine and Play + Learn™
and Parents Magazine Tip™ are
Trademarks of Gruner + Jahr
USA Publishing Co., New York, NY

© 2002 Learning Horizons, Inc.
One American Road
Cleveland, Ohio 44144
Printed in Hong Kong

AN AMERICAN GREETINGS COMPANY

WIGGLY TOOTH

by Catherine Lukas

Illustrated by Stephen Schreiber

I felt a funny feeling
while drinking some juice.

The straw began to jiggle.
My tooth was loose!

I love to wiggle my tooth.
I move it side to side.

I wiggle it while I wash.

I wiggle it while I ride.

I wiggle it in the classroom.
The kids all think it's cool.

I wiggle it while we read.
It's the loosest tooth in school!

13

I wiggle it with my dog
when I take her for a walk.

14

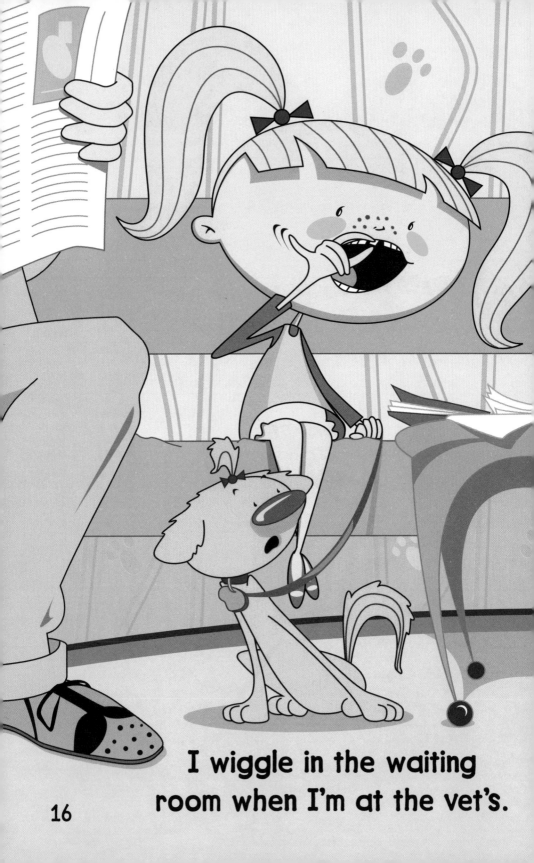

I wiggle in the waiting
room when I'm at the vet's.

I wiggle-wiggle-wiggle it
to entertain the pets.

My brother has big plans
for pulling my tooth out.

I cover up my mouth.
That makes my
brother shout.

I **like** my loose tooth
so I tell him, "Go away!"

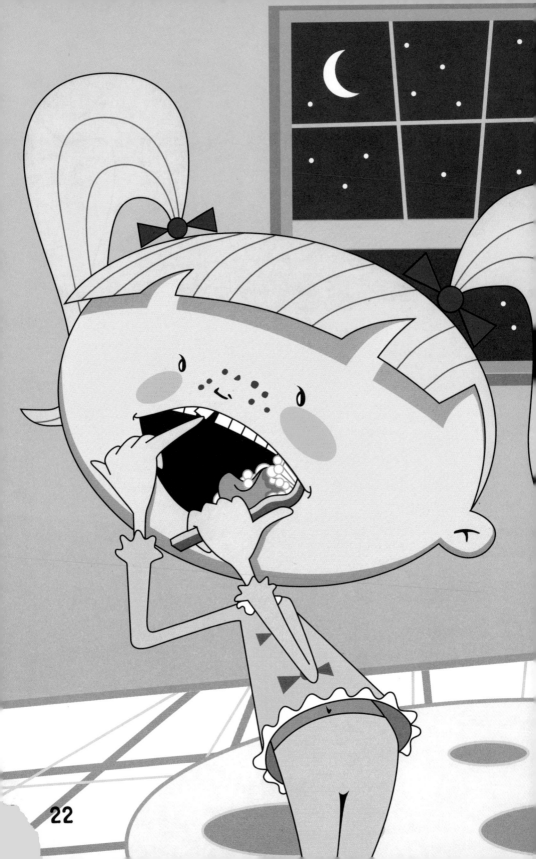

I want to wiggle-wiggle it
at least another day.

Now my tooth is looser.
I wiggle it in bed.

My brother comes to watch.
It's hanging by a thread!

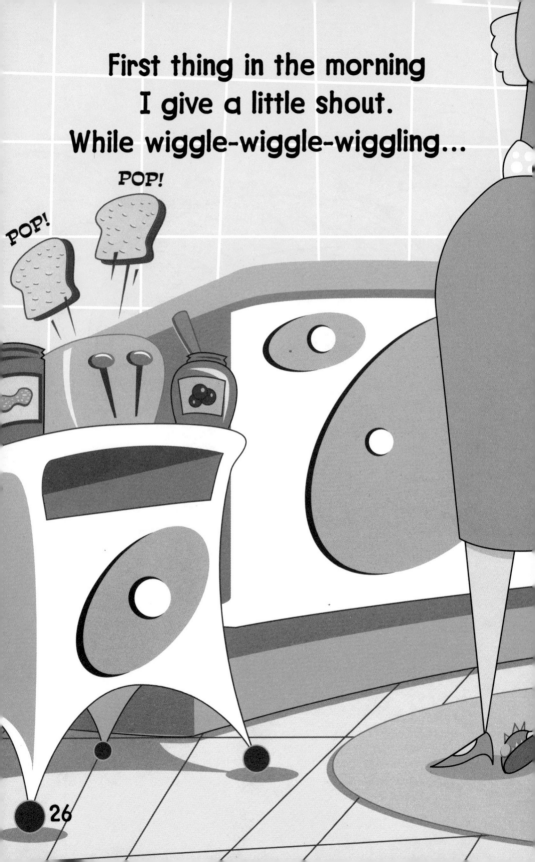

First thing in the morning
I give a little shout.
While wiggle-wiggle-wiggling...

POP!

POP!

POP!

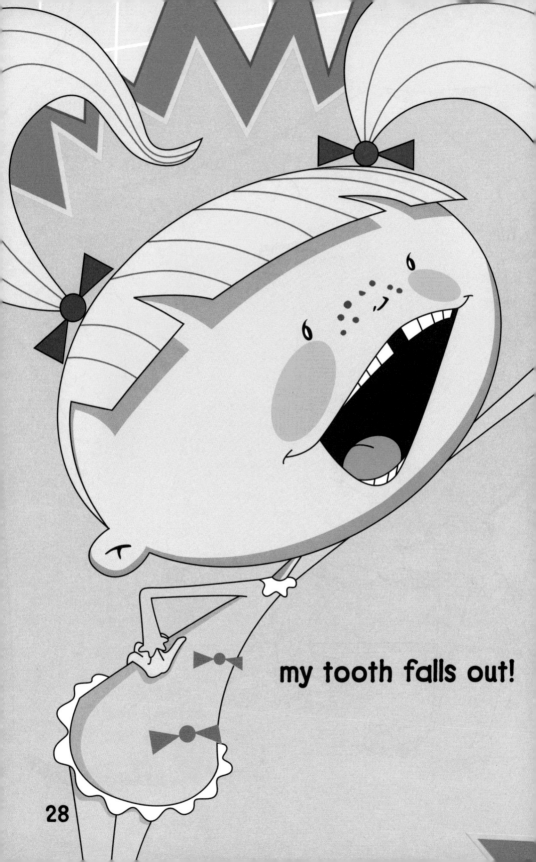

my tooth falls out!

29

Now my
tooth is missing.

Do you want to see?

31

EARLY SHAZAM!
DESIGN.

Frank